Dedication

I would like to dedicate this book to
God who gave me the words to write.

Also, to my editor the Late Franklin Russell Grill.

and finally to my mother who without her ghost
writing this story, it would have never been
transformed into a book.

Anna   Ricky

Chapter 1: An Evening at Dairy Lane

The evening was not a good time to go out and eat, as it arrived on the wings of fog mixed with a light mist wrapped around it. The coolness of the weather conjured images of a fireplace burning, reading a good book, and listening to the crackling of the fire. It made a person feel secure and comfortable. But tonight, plans were made for the gang to meet at the local Dairy Lane restaurant on Fredericksburg Island.

The gang consisted of four people who, how shall we say it, were mature individuals. There was Ricky Cambrose, a local farmer who enjoyed farming. With his sun-tanned skin and a perpetual smile, he often had a humorous story to share with family and friends. His wife, Anna, was more of the adventurous type. With her curious eyes and energetic spirit, she always found the mystery in things, and Ricky enjoyed her sense of adventure.

Next, there was Carl. Carl seemed to be the most quiet person of the bunch, which gave one the feel he may have had a secret past he didn't care to share with anyone. His reserved demeanor was complemented by a pair of wise, piercing eyes that seemed to always be evaluating the world around him.

Last, but not least, was Hattie, Carl's wife. Hattie, with her practical mindset and logical explanations, was the most factual one in the gang. Her calm voice and steady hands made her the perfect balance to Carl's quiet intensity.

As was mentioned earlier, the evening had a light settling mist with fog around it when the gang met at the local Dairy Lane. The restaurant was warm and inviting, the kind of place where the scent of freshly baked pies mingled with the sound of friendly chatter. The old wooden tables and checkered tablecloths added to its rustic charm.

As they sat around a table, Ricky got to laughing. His laughter was infectious and soon had everyone else smiling too. "This evening reminds me of a poem: "A frog sat in the rain, in his bum he had a pain, His demise he tried to feign, But no one's sympathy did he gain!""

Carl laughed heartily, his eyes crinkling at the corners. "That's funny!" He wiped his eyes with a napkin. "Ricky, how has your week been?" Carl asked, trying to change the subject.

"It's been good," Ricky replied, leaning back in his chair. "The crops are growing well, and I haven't had to treat pesty bugs yet. The new pigs I bought are getting along well and settling in great!"

"That man who dropped the pigs off," remarked Anna, tilting her head in thought, "stated he lived on the other side of the island, but I've never seen him before and neither has Ricky."

"He's probably new to the island, and we just haven't had the chance to meet him yet," commented Hattie. She took a sip of her drink before speaking again. While putting her sweater back on, she stated, "I find nights like this to be cozy and very comforting."

"I know, right," Anna said, her eyes lighting up. "I was just telling Ricky if we didn't need to be coming out to eat, I would stay home and read a book by the fireplace."

Carl, not listening to the women, asked, "What did this guy look like?"

"What guy are you talking about?" Ricky asked, having been distracted by the women's conversation.

"The guy that dropped off the pigs," Carl said, seeming a little annoyed at Ricky for having to ask such a question.

"Well, he was about my height, so about 6'1", and he has brown hair, and a stout face. He's not fat, but he's muscular. He looks like he's in his 30's."

"Did he tell you his name?" Carl asked.

Anna, still listening to the men's conversation, answered Carl's question. "He said something, but he mumbled; and Ricky and I didn't hear it, so we left it alone. He sure didn't look like anyone here on the island."

"Then he probably isn't related to anyone here," Hattie remarked.

The women continued to talk about the weather as the men resumed their discussion about farming.

"Here comes the food," Anna announced. Before anyone could say anything, she added, "These tacos look so good! I have been starving all day."

A moment later, Carl spoke up. "I feel like we should all get ice cream tonight. We need to celebrate the new pigs."

"We still haven't gotten all the pigs that I ordered. The man said he will bring the last two once they are fully weaned," Ricky commented.

"Well, I think we should get ice cream anyways," Carl announced, his eyes twinkling with mischief.

After dinner, it was time to say good-bye and leave to go home.

"It was good tonight. Thank you, Carl and Hattie, for going out to dinner with us. Anna and I enjoyed it!" said Ricky.

"Yep, Hattie and I had a good time too. It was good food," said Carl. "See you tomorrow," he added.

"Good night!" Ricky and Anna said together as the two couples left the restaurant.

While going home, Ricky observed, "It doesn't seem to want to let up."

"We will sleep good tonight with the raindrops falling on the roof," Anna said, smiling at the thought.

"Ricky, look out!" Anna yelled suddenly.

"Ugh!" Ricky stumbled and almost fell. "What did I trip over?" he asked, looking around in confusion.

"Hang on; let me get the flashlight." Anna looked quickly in her purse, finding the flashlight. As soon as the light shone on the body, she exclaimed, "It's a man!"

"A man? Is he all right? Bring the flashlight over here closer," Ricky commanded, his voice filled with concern.

"It's our pig deliverer! What happened to him?" Anna asked, her voice filled with worry.

"I don't know, but he's alive because he's breathing," Ricky replied, his voice steady. "Yell for Carl to come over here!" he added.

"Carl! Come over here! Ricky needs your help!" hollered Anna.

Carl's heavy footsteps could be heard running through the night air. "Who's that?" he asked, as he saw the body lying on the ground.

"It's the man that delivered our pigs. Help me pick him up and get him to our house," Ricky said, his tone urgent.

Carl   Hattie

Chapter 2: Unexpected Visitor

Anna knelt beside the unconscious man, gently shaking his shoulder. Her heart raced as she tried to keep her voice steady. "He's coming around. Can you hear us? Hello, are you okay?"

The man groaned and blinked his eyes open. "Uh... where am I?"

Ricky, standing nearby, offered a reassuring smile. "You're at our farm. I'm Ricky Cambrose, and this is my wife, Anna. Can you tell us what happened? Can you tell us your name?" Ricky's eyes were filled with concern, trying to mask his own rising anxiety.

The man winced, bringing a hand to his head. "Yeah, my name is Gordon Tower. My head hurts! I remember coming this evening to deliver those two last pigs I promised. I put them in the pen and shut the gate. Then... uh... my head hurts bad..." His voice trailed off, his face contorted in pain.

Without warning, Gordon's eyes rolled back, and he slumped to the ground once more.

"He passed out again," Ricky said with a note of urgency. "I sure wish the doctor would get here. He needs some help."

Anna glanced at the clock. She tapped her foot impatiently, feeling the weight of every second that ticked by. "It's been 20 minutes since I called Doctor White. It's a bad night to be out."

Carl, who had been standing nearby with his wife Hattie, stepped forward. "I guess there's nothing more for Hattie and me to do. I think we will be going home. Call me tonight if you need me. I'll come over and help. It's not like we live very far."

"Thank you for helping us with him," Anna said gratefully. "We'll call you if we need to. Good night. Be careful going home."

"Good night!" Carl and Hattie echoed before departing.

Anna stood up, brushing off her apron. "Well, I'm going to get a washcloth and wipe him off a bit. At least I can get his wounds cleaned up before Doctor White gets here."

"I'll get some coffee going. Doc may want some," Ricky offered, heading to the kitchen.

A knock at the door interrupted them, and Ricky opened it to reveal the doctor. "Hello, Doctor."

"Hello, Ricky. Your wife said you found an injured man."

"Yeah, I did. I fell over him coming home from the Dairy Lane this evening."

"Well, let's have a look, shall we?" Doctor White said, kneeling beside Gordon. "Well! Bless my soul! It's Vicar Tower!"

Ricky and Anna exchanged shocked glances. Anna's hand flew to her mouth in surprise. "Vicar Tower??!!" they exclaimed in unison.

Anna's eyes widened. "He's a pastor??!"

Doctor White chuckled. "Well, your new pastor, to be precise!"

Ricky scratched his head. "I thought our new pastor was due to be here in two months from now."

"He was," Doctor White explained. "But Pastor Tower was anxious to get here and meet everyone, so he came early and rented a farm on the other side of the island. Since he isn't getting paid yet from the church, he knows how to grow pigs and bees. So that's what he is doing. I will call Dorie, his wife, and tell her he is here and safe. She will be worried on a night like this."

"That would be a good idea," Anna agreed.

"Let me check him out to see what's going on here." Doctor White examined Gordon carefully. "He's coming around again... Pastor Tower, how are you feeling?"

Gordon groaned. "Like I got ran over by a Mac truck."

"I know. I checked you out though, and I think you just got off easy with that bump on your head. You'll be alright. Do you remember what happened?"

Gordon nodded slowly. "I came over to drop off the two pigs, and after I shut the gate, I turned to leave and someone or something came up from behind and hit me. I fell down in the dark and I hit my head. I don't remember anything else."

Ricky added, " You hit a stone wall. I found you on the side of our road facedown, and your head was by the stone wall that divides our pastures."

"Well, that explains what hit his head," Doctor White noted.

"Pastor Tower, let's move you off the couch to our guest bedroom. You will be more comfortable there," Anna suggested. "Plus, there's a bathroom where you can take a shower and get the grime off your scratches. I'll get some of Ricky's night clothes, and you can wear them tonight. I'll wash your clothes. Have you eaten dinner tonight?"

"Yes, I ate before I came, but can I have some water?" Gordon asked.

"Sure, we will get you some," Ricky said, handing over a glass of water. "Ok, Doctor, thank you for coming over. We'll make him comfortable tonight and wait for his wife to come in the morning. Thank you for everything you've done."

"It was my pleasure," Doctor White said, packing up his bag. "I didn't have much going on tonight anyway. Well, you folks have a good night. And Pastor Tower, don't do anything strenuous for the next few days. You should be fine."

"Good night, Doctor. Be careful going home," Anna and Ricky said in unison.

Gordon got cleaned up and settled into bed. Meanwhile, Ricky and Anna had a private moment in the kitchen.

"What's wrong, honey? I noticed that you were very quiet tonight," Ricky asked gently.

Anna sighed. She looked down, wringing her hands. "I guess I feel guilty and ashamed. I thought that Pastor Tower might've been someone who was not to my preference. Since I didn't know who he was, I never thought he would be our pastor. And I should have shown him more kindness in the beginning."

Ricky took her hand. "Hey, it's alright. Oh, that's what's going on. Well, sometimes you just can't judge a book by its cover. But you have a good heart, and I know that you're a very caring person. Don't get too upset; it will be alright."

Anna nodded, resting her head on Ricky's shoulder. "Thanks, huney. I wonder who or what it was that hit him and knocked him down..."

Chapter 3: A New Day

"I am so happy that we have blue skies this morning," Anna said, getting up and looking out the window. The morning sun streamed through the glass, casting a warm glow across the room. "What a contrast from last night. It feels as if the whole world is awake and happy this morning!" Ricky and Anna got dressed, and then Anna started the coffee brewing. The aroma filled the kitchen, adding to the cheerful atmosphere.

"Good morning!" Pastor Tower said as he came into the kitchen. He looked much better than the night before, his eyes clearer and his step steadier.

"Good morning!" Ricky and Anna said together. They were happy to see their guest had recovered well from the hit on the head.

"How are you feeling today?" Ricky asked the pastor.

"Much better. My head still hurts but not as bad as last night. This whole thing has given me something good to talk about!"

"What's that, Pastor?" Anna asked, her curiosity piqued.

"The title for my next sermon: 'Sin Can Hit You Hard and Make You Lose Your Senses!'"

Everyone laughed, the sound of their laughter mingling with the morning birdsong outside.

"Have you thought about what it could have been that hit you last night?" Ricky asked, pouring his guest a cup of coffee.

"You know, I've been thinking about that. It had to be a live creature or a human, because it ran off as I was falling. I heard its footsteps. But I don't know what it was or why it was out on a night like that," the pastor replied, his brow furrowing in thought.

"Did it make a verbal sound, that you can remember?" Ricky asked, handing him the coffee.

"No, all I remember is it was running, and it knocked me down."

"That's pretty strange," Ricky said, rubbing his forehead thoughtfully. "But I have been noticing other strange things happening around here too, like things missing. Just small things and then they are returned the next day."

"Well! It can't be anything bad, we do live on an island and not too many people live here!" Anna said, trying to reassure them all.

"Yep! Well, it's a bright day out today! And the daffodils are blooming, and the sun is out with blue skies, and the birds are singing; so, let's enjoy some breakfast!" Anna announced, her optimism infectious.

Ricky and Gordon agreed, and everyone smiled. "Okay."

Anna made a big breakfast for the three of them. After the hearty meal, Gordon rubbed his tummy

contently. "Now, that was a good breakfast!
Home-made bread, fried eggs, bacon, and
coffee!"

"Thank you, dear," Ricky said, getting up and
walking over to his wife to give her a kiss. He
emphasized what Gordon had just said. "That
was a very good breakfast!"

"Well, thank you guys! It was good," Anna
replied, pleased with their appreciation.

"Pastor, would you like to see the whole farm
before your wife gets here?" Ricky asked as
they were about to get up from the table.

"A walk around would be the right thing to do,"
Gordon agreed, patting his stomach. "I need to
walk off some of this food. I'm full."

"Would you two like a cup of coffee to go with
you?" Anna offered.

"Sure," the pastor said as he put on his coat.
Ricky chimed in, putting on his coat and hat,
"Yes, please."

As they stepped outside, Ricky took a deep
breath. "Ah... fresh air feels so good. "I enjoy it
out here."

There is a peacefulness to this place," the preacher said, taking in the serene surroundings.

"Come look at the new cattle barn we just had built," Ricky said, with joy in his voice.

"This is pretty nice! This barn should last you a hundred years or so," the pastor commented, admiring the sturdy construction.

"When we had it built, I made sure I got in a crew that builds stone barns the old way. It should last us beyond our years here," Ricky said proudly.

The men continued their tour of the barn until Pastor Tower spotted someone in the distance. "Oh! I see my wife now. Hello, Dorie, I'm over here!" he called out, waving.

Dorie walked quickly towards her husband, her face filled with relief. "Hello! How are you feeling, dear?" she asked, her hands reaching out to touch his face.

"Doctor White said for me to take it easy for a few days and I should be fine. The bump on my head still hurts, but I guess I should expect that," Gordon replied.

"Good," Dorie said softly, her hands still on his face.

"Here, Ricky," the pastor said, "I'll give the cup of coffee back to you. Thank your wife for us, please."

"Sure will! Take it easy now. Don't overdo it," Ricky cautioned.

"I won't, promise!" the pastor replied.

"Would you and your wife like to come over this Saturday evening for dinner?" Dorie asked. "I would like to make dinner for you and thank you for helping Gordon out."

"Well, thank you; yes, we would!" Ricky replied, smiling.

"Six p.m. Will that be fine?" Dorie asked.

"Six it is! Would you like us to bring anything?" Ricky offered.

"No, I'll have it all ready for you," Dorie replied.

Gordon and Dorie said their goodbyes. Ricky waved back at them as they got into their buggy and started down the road.

Chapter 4: A Day on the Island

With the new pigs adapting to their pens at Cambrose Farm and the vegetables growing healthy in the garden, Ricky and Anna felt that work could wait for now. This was a day to get out and enjoy themselves.

"Why don't we get on our bikes and go bicycling around the island?" Ricky suggested, his eyes sparkling with excitement.

Anna's face lit up with a broad smile. "Okay, that sounds like fun," she replied, her tone filled with eagerness.

Ricky, a tall, rugged man with a perpetual farmer's tan, got the bikes out of the shed and dusted them off. It didn't take his wife long to prepare a picnic lunch and place it in a basket. Anna, with her sun-kissed hair tied back in a ponytail, was efficient and quick on her feet.

As they leisurely traveled down the dirt road, Anna noticed how beautiful the colors of the different flowers looked. The island was in full bloom, and the grass was a vibrant green against the blue sky and the glistening ocean. The scent of wildflowers filled the air, and the sounds of nature added a soothing background melody.

"You know, Ricky, we live on a pretty island! The blooming rose bushes and the green trees make the stone houses look beautiful! Even the birds are singing loudly today," she remarked, her voice filled with appreciation.

Ricky, glancing at his wife with affection, nodded in agreement. "It's like a little paradise," he said, his voice carrying a note of contentment.

As they pedaled and talked, all the while taking in the scenery as they rode, they finally came to the oceanfront, where the beach looked so inviting. The waves gently lapped at the shore, and the sun cast a golden glow over the sand.

"Feel that breeze," Anna remarked, closing her eyes and taking a deep breath. "Doesn't that feel good?"

"Let's eat our lunch here," Ricky suggested, his voice filled with enthusiasm.

"Okay, let's go to that table over there by the tree. We can see the ocean much better from there," Anna pointed out, her eyes scanning the area for the perfect spot.

As she spread the tablecloth on the wooden table and then laid out the food of sandwiches, chips, and lemonade, with cookies for dessert, Ricky began to tell her the history of the island. He spoke with a tone of intrigue, hoping to pique Anna's interest.

"Do you know right where you are standing there used to be a fort back in the day?" Ricky said to Anna, his eyes twinkling with curiosity. "I guess there were pirate ships that liked to come to this island, so the military set up a fort right here. They say there are tunnels and buried treasure on the island, but I've lived here my whole life and never found any of the treasures."

The two sat down to eat, the aroma of fresh sandwiches wafting through the air.

"Ah, buried treasure, like diamond tiaras, jewels, and gold coins?" Anna questioned with hope in her voice, her eyes wide with excitement.

"Well, that is what the legends and stories say. I do know there was an old military fort here. In fact, right where this table is, used to be where one of the cannons sat," Ricky replied, his voice tinged with a hint of mystery.

"Have you ever found any of the tunnels?" Anna asked, her curiosity piqued.

"No, and I have been all over this island as a little kid. I've never seen one," Ricky said, with disappointment in his voice.

Anna changed the subject, not wanting to dwell on Ricky's disappointment. "Look! There is a small red boat coming towards the shore." On a day like today, with the blueness of the ocean and the red boat, it just makes that boat so pretty." The person pulled up to shore further down the beach from where Ricky and Anna were eating their lunch. "Isn't that Carl getting off the boat?" Anna asked, squinting to get a better look.

"Yeah, it looks like him," Ricky responded, shading his eyes with his hand.

They continued to eat as the water splashed against the shoreline and the seagulls flew around, singing their songs. Ricky and Anna finished their picnic lunch at the table in their bare feet, the sand cool and soothing. After eating, they just sat there listening to the waves and the seagulls and just about fell asleep. Suddenly, Anna thought that they had better start heading home.

"Where did Carl go?" Anna wondered out loud. "We saw him walking up the beach. But I do not see him now."

"I don't know." Ricky turned his bike around to head back home. "Well, you about ready to go home?" he asked, looking at Anna with a smile.

"Yeah, I got to get home and water the garden. It's starting to look good now, with all the vegetables coming up," Anna replied, standing up and stretching.

Ricky suggested, "Come on, I'll race you home!"

Anna was still thinking about Carl. "I wonder where Carl went?" She questioned as she kicked her stand loose from the sand to turn her bike around and start pedaling to catch up to Ricky.

Because it was all uphill to go home, she knew that she would have to pedal hard trying to catch up to Ricky, as he was quite a way up the road.

On the other side of the island, where Ricky and Anna had had their lunch, Carl was walking up to the preacher's house. "Hello, Pastor Tower!" he addressed, waving as he approached.

"Hello!" Vicar Tower responded, a warm smile on his face.

"How are you feeling today?" Carl asked, as he arrived at where the preacher was sitting outside enjoying the sounds of the island. He sat down in the offered chair by the round table. "I helped Ricky pick you up off the ground when you hit your head," he said, placing the parcel that he was carrying on the table. "I have this package for you, so I came over here to give it to you. I figured you would be needing this."

Vicar Tower was glad to get the box. "Oh, thank you. Yes, I ordered that a month ago. Did it come into the post office here on the island already?" he asked, his eyebrows raised in surprise.

"No, I was on the mainland today, and I saw this in their post office for you when I picked up the mail for the islanders. So, I came to give it to you and to check up to see how you were feeling," Carl explained, sitting back in his chair.

"Oh!" he laughed. "I'm doing much better, thank you. I'm sorry but I don't remember your name," the vicar said, a look of apology on his face.

"You were hit hard. My name is Carl, my wife is Hattie. We live on a farm near Ricky and Anna's farm," Carl explained with a friendly smile.

The two men talked for quite a while before the vicar's guest stood up to leave.

The pastor rose from his chair and said, "We invited Ricky and Anna to come to supper for Saturday night. Would you and Hattie like to come and eat with us as well?" Pastor Tower asked.

"That would be nice, thank you. We will see you soon! Have a blessed day!" Carl said before heading to his farm. Pastor Tower shook Carl's hand and said, "See you soon. Bye!"

Chapter 5: Mysteries on the Farm

The bright sunlight of the next morning greeted Ricky and Anna as they walked outside. Ricky, a sturdy man with a friendly demeanor, squinted and asked, "Anna, have you seen Clucky, the chicken?"

Anna shook her head, her ponytail swaying. "No, I haven't. She's probably off somewhere chasing bugs to eat. Have you seen my garden hoe?"

"No, I haven't seen it, but it will turn up soon; don't worry," Ricky replied reassuringly, with a smile that conveyed his usual optimism.

"Things just seem to come up missing a lot lately. But then we find them later. I guess we are just getting too old—forgetting where we put the stuff," Anna commented with a chuckle, her eyes twinkling with humor.

Anna glanced around the yard by the house, taking in the vibrant colors of the flowers she had planted against the stone fence. Often, she would look up at the sky and admire it. "The sky is so blue, and the flowers I planted sure are pretty up against the stone fence. Ahh... It feels like a happy day," she mused, smiling to herself. She loved their farm; it was so peaceful, and a person could be content to live there for the rest of their life.

"I found Clucky," Ricky announced with a grin. "She has a nest in the back of the barn. I also found your garden hoe next to her. I guess you forgot to put it up."

"Well, I guess I did, but I thought for sure I had put it up," Anna responded, shaking her head in mild disbelief.

Ricky and Anna enjoyed their gardening and chores around the house and barn. Work didn't seem like work to them on the farm. Later in the day, Carl came over.

"Hey, Ricky!" Carl called out as he approached. "I thought I would come over and ask for help. I had a big pine tree come down near the house last night from the strong wind. I was wondering if I could get your help cleaning it up."

"Sure. I would be glad to help. Let me grab my chainsaw, and I will walk with you," Ricky said, nodding.

"Okay," responded Carl with a relieved smile.

As they walked through the pasture, Ricky noticed some footprints in the field of hay going towards Carl's farm. "That's strange," he murmured to himself.

"What's strange?" Carl asked, overhearing his friend.

"These footprints—they seem to come from my place and go straight for your farm," Ricky explained, pointing at the ground.

Carl stopped and studied the footprints. "Yeah, they do. Let's get over there and see if someone has been messing around my place."

Both men quickly made their way over to Carl's farm, their pace quickening with concern.

"Hattie! Hattie!" Carl called out as they approached the house.

"What?" Hattie responded from inside, her voice slightly muffled.

"Have you seen anyone or anything around here today?" Carl asked, his voice raised in concern as he scanned the area.

"No, but I've been busy canning some stuff from the garden," Hattie replied, coming to the door with a puzzled look.

"Let's look around and see if we can locate what it can be," Ricky suggested, glancing around the property.

"Yeah, I don't like to think of anyone here snooping around my property," Carl said, frowning as he clenched his fists.

After a while of scouring the property, Ricky asked, "Have you noticed anything?"

Carl stopped and said, "No, everything looks good to me. Nothing is out of place either."

"Let's get that tree taken care of," Ricky suggested, shifting the focus back to the task at hand.

While the men were busy over at Carl and Hattie's place, Anna was working in her garden. The garden was a vibrant patchwork of vegetables and flowers, with neatly tended rows and a sense of order and care. She noticed several crows flying around.

"Oh, good gravy! The crows are back. I guess I will need to put up a scarecrow in my garden so they won't eat my corn," she said in frustration, shaking her head as she watched the crows circle above.

Chapter 6: The Mysteries of Dairy Lane

As the late afternoon sun dipped below the horizon in Fredericksburg, Ricky and Anna prepared to go out for dinner. The cozy little island, known for its historic charm and friendly faces, had been their home for years. Ricky, searching high and low in their quaint farm house, asked, "Honey, where is my pocketknife; have you seen it?"

Anna, equally puzzled, replied, "No, I haven't, but have you seen my bracelet? I know I left it here on the dresser." Frustration crept into her voice. "This is getting frustrating! I wanted to wear it to the Dairy Lane for dinner tonight."

Ricky pondered for a moment, then asked, "Do you have a spooky feeling about the stuff that keeps on vanishing around here?"

Anna sighed, her blue eyes reflecting her annoyance. "I know I am frustrated! Are we really getting that old, where we misplace things all the time?"

Ricky, with a playful glint in his eye and a swagger that told his age, strutted around the room. "Well, personally, I'm still young and handsome, but you might be getting that old. I don't know." He teased.

Anna glared at him, feigning laughter. "Ha ha ha, you're so funny," she said sarcastically. "Twenty thousand comedians out of work, and you crack a joke. Let's go eat."

They stepped into the warm glow of the late afternoon sun and headed for the Dairy Lane. The small-town eatery was a favorite among locals, with its retro decor and mouth-watering comfort food. Upon arrival, they met their friends Carl and Hattie. After everyone was comfortably seated at the table, the men started conversing.

"Thank you, Ricky, for helping me with cutting that tree down," Carl said. "Now I have firewood."

"Glad to help. I just wish I could figure out what made the footprints going to your property," Ricky commented.

"What footprints?" Anna asked, her curiosity piqued.

Hattie interjected, "Oh, the guys found footprints that led from your property to ours."

"Human footprints or animals?" Anna inquired.

"I don't know; it was mostly indentations in the grass leading to their place," Ricky replied.

Hattie, with a hint of fear in her voice, said, "Maybe it was from whoever knocked Pastor Tower down last week. That would mean whoever that was, was at our property as we walked back home in the dark." Anna looked intently at her friend, concern etched on her face.

Ricky attempted to lighten the mood by reciting a poem. "To start, a man sat in the dark, till his wife came in and turned on the lights…"

Anna interrupted. "You're just full of it tonight, aren't you? It didn't even rhyme."

"I know, I couldn't think of anything to say except fart, so I made it nicer," he admitted, chuckling.

They all laughed, and Hattie spoke up. "Okay, when we walk home tonight, nothing is going to happen, right?"

"Right, I agree. Let's eat and enjoy the dinner," Anna said, as the waitress arrived with their order.

"Oh! Carl," Anna said, taking a bite out of her taco, "Ricky and I saw you on the beach two days ago, but you disappeared; where did you go?"

"I had things to do," Carl said mysteriously. "So, I didn't hang around."

Ricky and Anna raised their eyebrows in unison as they looked at each other.

"Man! Can the food get any better here?" Carl said loudly, causing several heads to turn.

"I had a very good supper," Hattie agreed with her husband.

Ricky added, "My stomach is full," as he patted his belly. "Yep, they cook good here."

"I'm ready for dessert," Anna chimed in. "Any of you want some cheesecake?"

Ricky groaned, implying he couldn't eat any more, and Carl and Hattie shook their heads.

After more small talk, Ricky rose from his chair and announced, "Well, it's time to go home." He lowered his voice. "Hey, before we go, I had a thought. Since we're all going to Pastor Tower's house for supper tomorrow evening, do you want to ride in the wagon together?"

They all agreed that it would be a good idea.

"Okay, then I will hitch up the mules to our hay wagon," he said enthusiastically.

As Anna and Ricky were walking home through the darkened road of their neighborhood, Anna said, "It sure is dark out here. I can hardly see where to walk."

Ricky offered his arm to Anna. "Hang on to my arm, and if we fall, we fall together," he said.

Anna realized they hadn't said goodnight to their friends. "Goodnight, Carl and Hattie!" she called softly.

Carl and Hattie responded in unison, "Goodnight."

Suddenly, Ricky pulled on Anna's arm and said, "Stop!"

"What?" she asked.

"Shhhh!" he cautioned.

Anna looked around, whispering, "What?"

Ricky whispered back, "There is someone or something in front of us, moving in the tree line."

"Carl," Ricky called in a loud whisper, motioning for his friend to join him. "Come here. Do you see something moving in the tree line past my buildings?"

"Yep, I do. It's something big. It can't be a man," Carl observed.

By this time, Hattie was standing beside her husband. "I'm getting sick and tired of all this!" she announced loudly. "HEY! YOU THERE! STOP!"

The big creature started running away when Hattie yelled at it.

"Way to go, Hattie," Carl said. "Now we won't find out what it is."

"I'm with Hattie," Anna announced. "I'm getting sick and tired of all this crazy, scary stuff that's been going on lately. This is a peaceful island, not a spine-chilling island."

"Way to go, Hattie!" Carl said again.

"Well, whispering about it wasn't getting anything done," Hattie reminded him.

"Nope," Anna agreed.

"Come on, guys, time to get home and go to bed," Ricky announced.

"Crazy women," the men muttered under their breath as they went their separate ways

Chapter 7: A New Day Dawns

Anna, a woman with a curious mind and an adventurous spirit, gazed out of her bedroom window as the new day dawned. The clear, blue sky stretched endlessly above, and the gentle breeze from the ocean brought the scent of salt and freedom. Birds sang a symphony, welcoming the morning.

Ricky, her kind-hearted and resourceful husband, called out from the kitchen, "Honey, come here. I have solved one of our mysteries, and I think you will be happy," his voice filled with excitement.

Anna, finishing the last touch on her hair, responded with a playful smile, "What mystery is that?"

"Just come with me and I'll show you," Ricky replied, a twinkle of mischief in his eyes.

He took Anna's hand and led her to the barn. The scent of hay and the soft light filtering through the wooden slats created a serene atmosphere. They climbed up into the hayloft, where dust motes danced in the air.

"As I was pitching hay down to the bottom floor this morning," Ricky began, "I looked up and noticed a crow sitting on a nest in the crook of the ceiling beam. So, I got the ladder and looked inside her nest to see the babies. But guess what I found instead?"

Anna's eyes widened with curiosity. "What?" she asked eagerly, her heart pounding with anticipation.

"Climb up there and see for yourself," Ricky said, holding the ladder steady.

Anna carefully climbed the ladder, her fingers trembling with excitement. "Hey! There's my bracelet! And your pocketknife! Wait, there's something else in the nest." She reached further into the nest and picked up two gold coins, her eyes shining with amazement. "What are these?"

Ricky climbed up to join her, taking the coins from her hands. "Let me see." He examined them closely, turning them over and over. "They are two Spanish coins. They are old!"

Anna's eyes sparkled with excitement. "I guess there is buried treasure on this island after all, and the crow knows where it is!"

"Huh. I guess so," Ricky replied, a thoughtful look on his face. "Let's take all this to the house."

Anna nodded, her mind racing with possibilities. "I forgot crows like shiny things," she said as they headed back to their cozy home. "Well, that's one mystery solved. From now on, we will keep our bedroom window closed until the crow is gone."

"Yeah, I think so too. Let me look at the coins again," Anna said, her curiosity unabated.

Ricky handed them over with a smile. "I wonder where the crow found these coins," Anna mumbled to herself, a sense of adventure igniting in her heart.

The next day, Hattie, a warm and diligent woman with a heart full of faith, went to the church down the street. The old church stood as a beacon of hope, its stained glass windows casting colorful reflections inside. She cleaned the sanctuary for the upcoming service, her movements graceful and purposeful.

As she worked, she began to sing, her voice echoing through the empty church. "Bringing in the sheaves, bringing in the sheaves, we shall come rejoicing bringing in the sheaves," she sang, then paused with a chuckle. "Or is it sheep?" she asked herself, her laughter filling the sacred space. "Either way, we are bringing them in. Oh, what a day it will be."

She continued singing another hymn, her voice filled with reverence. "Oh, what a day that will be when my Jesus I shall see. When I look upon His face. The one who saved me by His grace, when He takes me by the hand and leads me through the Promised Land. What a day... glorious day... that will be."

"Hello! Hello! Is there anyone here?" Dadel's voice echoed through the church. Dadel, a dedicated church secretary with a kind smile, always printed the bulletins for the services.

Hattie hollered back with a grin, "Hello, Dadel! It's just me cleaning the church for Sunday's service."

"I know; I heard. That was some pretty singing you were doing!" Dadel said as she entered, her eyes twinkling.

Hattie laughed. "Hahahahaha. I guess I was in the mood to sing a few songs. Is it bringing in the sheaves or is it bringing in the sheep? What is a sheave, do you know?"

"I've been a church secretary for over 35 years," Dadel replied, "I don't know. Let's go look in the dictionary and see what a sheave is." The ladies headed to the office, their curiosity piqued. "By the way, the song is Bringing in the Sheaves," she announced with a smile, "not sheep."

Hattie nodded thoughtfully. "I know what you mean, sister Dadel. Both sound good to me though. Sheaves mean cereal crops, like wheat, it would be a bundle, the sheaves, so I guess we are singing about the spiritual crop God has. Bringing in the sheaves to heaven."

"That sounds about right!" Dadel agreed, her eyes shining with understanding.

Suddenly, Dadel remembered why she had come. "I just came here to drop off the bulletins for Sunday," she said, placing them on the small table in the entryway.

"Just let me finish up with dusting here and I will leave with you," Hattie said, her hands moving quickly and efficiently.

As Hattie dusted the back bead-board-wall, she pressed a little too hard, and part of it opened up! "Dadel, look, a trap door!" she exclaimed, her voice filled with surprise.

Dadel hurried over, peering into the darkness beyond the door. "Wooooh," both women whispered, their eyes wide with wonder.

Dadel moved closer to Hattie and whispered, "Are you going down those stairs?"

"Nope. I believe I'm just going to let this be. How about you?" Hattie replied, her voice steady.

"I think we should agree on this. Let's let this be," Dadel concurred with a nod.

"I'm going home. I have a dinner to go to this evening," Hattie said, dusting off her hands.

"I'm going home, too. I have to fix dinner," Dadel said, a smile playing on her lips.

Later that afternoon, Ricky, ever the determined farmer, announced, "I better go to the barn and hitch up Barthlamule and Muletilda to the hay wagon," as he put on his well-worn hat and headed outside.

Anna, her hands on her hips, protested, "We are taking those two tonight?! Why?" her voice tinged with annoyance.

Ricky, not one to back down, responded, "Now that's not fair. They have been good lately; I've been working with them. I say we take the mules tonight."

Anna, recalling a previous mishap, whined, "But last time we were with them, they bit my derriere!"

"Well, it was your fault!" Ricky retorted, a mischievous grin spreading across his face.

"No! It wasn't!" Anna shouted, her cheeks flushing with indignation.

Ricky's hearty laughter filled the air. "Yes it was! You sewed on your back pockets a big carrot, and the other one had an apple sewed on it!"

Anna crossed her arms, her face still red. "But they didn't smell them! They were cloth patches!"

Ricky shook his head, still laughing. "They obviously know what they like when they see it.

And those are big patches!" he pointed out, doubling over with laughter.

Anna couldn't help but smile. "Well, they have a lot of territories to cover," she said, defending herself.

"I'm hooking up the mules," Ricky announced, wiping tears of laughter from his eyes as he hurried to the barn.

Meanwhile, at Carl and Hattie's place, the couple was getting ready to leave for dinner. Hattie spoke up as she put on her jacket, "Carl, when I was cleaning the church today, I was dusting the back wall panel and ..."

Carl, ever practical, interrupted, "Hattie, you need to get dressed, we will be leaving soon! I'm going out to make sure everything is locked up."

"Well!" Hattie mumbled to herself, adjusting her jacket that was decorated with playful apple and carrot patches.

Ricky wasn't through talking about the mules. "Now, I just want you to know," he said as he and Anna were about to get on the wagon, "I have been working with Barthlamule and Muletilda on their manners. I showed them what a real carrot and apple smell and taste like. I think they will mind their manners tonight. Plus, I dressed them up real nice tonight. I put a hat on Tillie because she likes to look pretty, and I put a big tie on Bartie. He is feeling pretty handsome tonight!"

Anna rolled her eyes, a smile tugging at her lips. "I am not going to be wearing any food patches on me just to make sure," she retorted.

"That's a good idea. My lady, your chariot awaits," Ricky said with a playful bow as Anna climbed into the wagon.

Chapter 8: The Hayride and the Hidden Treasure

"Hello!" Pastor Tower called out as the two couples arrived at his house. His voice was warm and welcoming, fitting his role as the spiritual leader of the community. His tall frame and gentle demeanor put everyone at ease. "Did you have a good hayride over here?" he asked, his eyes twinkling with genuine interest. "Yes, it was very nice," they all agreed, smiling at the familiar, comforting presence of their pastor.

As the passengers got down from the wagon, Pastor Tower spoke to Ricky, a man known for his reliability and calm nature. "Ricky, after everyone gets down from the wagon, you can unhitch the mules and put them in the barn if you like," he instructed. "Okay, thank you," Ricky replied, nodding appreciatively. "Here Ricky, I'll help you," Carl suggested as he overheard what the preacher said to his friend. Carl was a sturdy man, always ready to lend a hand and quick with a laugh.

As the girls stepped inside the house, they were greeted by the cozy aroma of home-cooked food. The Tower's home was modest but filled with warmth, its wooden beams and rustic décor reflecting the simplicity and love that defined the couple.

"Hello Mrs. Tower," Anna said. Anna, with her kind eyes and gentle smile, was always thoughtful and caring. "I would like to introduce you to Hattie. She is Carl's wife." "Hello," Mrs. Tower said, wiping her hands on her apron before extending one to Hattie. "Just call me Dorie. Nice to meet you, Hattie. Did you have a wonderful hayride over here?" "Oh, yes! And it's just a lovely evening for one," Hattie commented, her eyes shining with excitement.

Hattie's lively spirit was contagious, and she had a way of making everyone feel included. "It is fun to get out and take a ride every once in a while," Anna remarked, her voice soft but cheerful.

Mrs. Tower let the women know what was on the menu since the men hadn't come in yet. "I hope you all are hungry. I made barbecue ribs, corn on the cob, salad, mashed potatoes with gravy, homemade rolls, sweet tea, and Keylime cheesecake for dessert."

It was more than Hattie could keep to herself and she let out a "Wow! That sounds so good!" Hattie's enthusiasm was palpable, and it brought a smile to everyone's faces. "Yes, it does!" Anna said, "Can we help you with anything?" she asked. "Nope," Dorie said, smiling. "I think we are ready to sit down and eat as soon as the guys get in here."

"Sure smells good in here," Ricky said as the men came through the door. He softly sniffed the air, savoring the delicious aroma. "I was just about to say that," Carl interjected, chuckling. "Dorie has been cooking up a storm today," her husband, Gordon, said, looking at his wife with pride. Gordon, a robust man with a hearty laugh, always appreciated Dorie's culinary skills. "I just wanted to thank you all for helping my husband," she said, smiling at him. "It means so much to me; so, this is my way of thanking you." "You're welcome, we were so glad to help both of you out," Ricky said, his sincerity evident in his tone.

Dorie dished up the food and placed it before the hungry group.

"Let's say grace," Pastor Tower suggested, his voice calming and authoritative. He removed his napkin from under his plate and spread it on his lap. Everyone bowed their heads. "Lord, we thank you for the help you sent me the other day, and, Lord, we thank you so much for all this wonderful food. In your Holy name, Amen." The group said, "Amen," in unison, their voices filled with gratitude.

It didn't take the guests long to dig into the tasty food that they put on their plates. Everyone was busy eating because there wasn't much talk going on.

Ricky was halfway through his meal when he asked, "After dinner, would everyone like to take a hayride? Then we can come back for dessert." His suggestion was met with enthusiasm. They all liked the suggestion. "Sure! Sounds great!" they said one after another.

After everyone was finished and their stomachs were full, Hattie and Anna helped Dorie to put the leftover food in the refrigerator and take the dirty dishes to the dishwasher. Dorie put the soap in the dishwasher so it could be cleaning while they were on the hayride.

Ricky and Carl went out to hitch up the mules Tillie and Bart. After they were hitched to the wagon, they drove the wagon up to the door of the house. Ricky warned everyone while he helped the women climb on the wagon seat, "Be careful getting up on the wagon."

As Hattie moved past Barthlamule, she saw his head jerk and heard his teeth biting the air. "Did you just see that?" Hattie said nervously. "Bart just tried to bite me! Why is he acting like that? He's never acted like that around me before."

Anna said sarcastically, "Ricky, do you want to tell Hattie why Bart is treating her like that?" Now, Hattie was very curious, and she turned to look at Ricky with a puzzled look. Ricky got right to the point. "Hattie, it's your jacket." Hattie looked down at her jacket. "What's wrong with my jacket?" "Oh, now I understand," Carl said, cutting into the conversation while laughing. "Hattie, you have apples and carrots on your jacket. Bart thinks it's food." Everyone caught the joke and began to laugh with Carl.

"I brought the mules apples and carrots just in case they got hungry," Ricky said. Even though Ricky and Carl were laughing, they hurriedly fed the animals some apples and carrots.

After the incident with the mules, the evening didn't turn out too bad. It was delightful for everyone. "Ricky, can we ride by the ocean tonight?" Pastor Gordon asked. "It's so calm and the moon is full." Gordon's wife chimed in. "That would be so nice." "Sure," Ricky said. "It's a perfect evening for it. Let's go!"

Ricky steered the mules slowly by the ocean as they heard the water lapping at the shoreline. The moon was just coming up on the horizon, casting a silvery glow on the water. Gordon put his arm around his wife and gave her a squeeze. The two looked at each other and were lost in the moment. No one wanted this evening to end.

The Tower's charming farmhouse stood proudly against the backdrop of rolling hills, its porch light casting a welcoming glow. Ricky guided the mules to a halt in front of the Tower's door and securely tied them to the hitching post. The mules snorted and pawed at the ground, eager to rest. Once everyone dismounted from the wagon, they all made their way inside, greeted by the rich aroma of Keylime cheesecake. The farmhouse, with its cozy wooden interiors and the soft glow of lanterns, felt like a warm embrace.

Inside, they gathered around the wooden table, savoring the tangy sweetness of the cheesecake. Laughter filled the room as they reminisced about old times and shared stories. After their coffee and dessert, they longed to linger and chat, but it was getting late. Knowing they had a long journey home, the two couples bid their goodbyes and excused themselves for the night.

As the mules plodded along at a leisurely pace, the foursome settled comfortably in their seats, soaking in the tranquil evening ambiance. The rhythmic clip-clop of the mules' hooves and the gentle creak of the wagon created a soothing backdrop to their thoughts. The night was peaceful, with the moon casting a silvery glow over the landscape.

Before reaching the Stehling farm, they had to pass by the old stone church. Suddenly, they heard soft singing, the melody drifting through the night air.

"Ricky, stop the wagon!" Anna exclaimed, startled, her eyes wide with curiosity.

Ricky brought the wagon to a halt, the mules snorting in protest. Hattie, intrigued, leaned forward, her brow furrowed. "Is there someone in the church singing at this time of night?" she asked, her voice tinged with wonder.

Peering into the darkness, Anna noted, "All the lights in the church are off. I don't think...."

But Hattie interrupted her, her eyes sparkling with excitement. "Today when I was cleaning, I found a trap door in the back wall panel. Maybe they are singing under the church," she said, her voice dropping to a conspiratorial whisper.

Both men turned around to look at Hattie, disbelief etched on their faces. Carl, scratching his head, said, "It doesn't sound muffled like it's coming from under the church."

"It sounds like they are singing near the church," Ricky added, his brow furrowing as he listened.

As the men debated whether to investigate the source of the sound, they failed to notice the crow perched in the bell tower, illuminated by the moonlight. Its black feathers glistened as it watched them with beady eyes.

"It's just humming a song," Anna remarked, straining her ears. "Wait! Listen!!......."

They could now distinctly hear the words:

Talk of High. But you bow your head. Go down, down, around and around though instead. Ships come in but do not stay. In the vault does the treasure lay. Can you count once or twice But turn left and then right to look at the bay. Count your coins like a spy but look ahead do not think you can delay.

Hattie, feeling uneasy, wrapped her shawl tighter around her shoulders. "Okay! If things haven't been spooky enough lately, now we have a midnight singer," she said, her voice trembling slightly.

Anna, worried, turned to her husband, her eyes pleading. "Ricky, I want to go home. Get us home now, please!"

Ricky nodded, his jaw set. He tried to reassure them, "Don't let this scare you too much." He forced a smile. "The words were nice. They talked about hidden treasure. Maybe we can figure it out and become millionaires!"

Carl's eyes lit up at the thought. "What would we do with a million dollars?" he mused, a grin spreading across his face.

Hattie eagerly chimed in, "I would buy a nice big house."

Anna, still shaken, managed a laugh. "I would buy a pair of nice mules."

Ricky, slightly offended but amused, responded with a chuckle, "Hey! Hey!! That's not nice!"

Hattie, agreeing with Anna but with a playful twist, said, "Well, maybe I would buy your mules a nice soft muzzle, so when they get hungry and try to bite people wearing food on their clothes, they can't."

As the wagon rolled up to Carl and Hattie's door, Ricky announced, "Well, here we are."

Carl, grateful for the distraction from the eerie encounter, said, "Thank you for the hayride," as he helped his wife down from the wagon. "We had a great time."

Ricky and Anna bid them goodnight as Carl and Hattie reached their door. Turning back, Carl and Hattie waved and said goodnight once more before disappearing into the house

Chapter 9: Breakfast and Mysteries

The next morning, sunlight filtered through the curtains of the cozy farmhouse as Anna started making breakfast. The warm scent of fried eggs and pancakes filled the kitchen, mingling with the sweet aroma of syrup and freshly squeezed orange juice. Anna hummed a cheerful tune as she worked, her mind occupied with the day's plans.

Meanwhile, Ricky, always an early riser, headed out to the barn to feed the animals. He had a special bond with them and loved talking to them as if they were his pets. The morning air was crisp, and the sky was painted with hues of pink and orange as the sun began its ascent.

"Good morning, chickens! Do you want some food?" Ricky called out, scattering grain into their feeders. The chickens cackled back, their feathers ruffling as they eagerly pecked at the grain.

After ensuring the chickens were satisfied, Ricky moved to the pigs. He leaned over the fence and grinned, "Good morning, pigs! Did you have a good night's sleep?" The pigs responded with delighted oinks, their little tails wagging in anticipation.

Next, Ricky approached the mules, Tillie and Bart. The large animals stood patiently in their enclosure, their ears flicking as they heard his voice. "Gooood morning, you two! Thanks for taking us on the hayride last night! Did you have fun like we did? We sure did," he said, patting Tillie's neck affectionately. As Ricky bent over to put the feed in their trough, Bart unexpectedly bit him on the rear.

"Ow!" Ricky yelped, standing up abruptly. "Hey now! You turkey! Why did you do that!? Stop that! Here is your feed. Right here in the trough. Not back there!" He rubbed his backside, feeling the throbbing pain from the bite. Frustrated and hurt, he decided to return to the house, questioning whether Anna was right about selling the mules.

Inside, Anna was bustling around the kitchen, plating the breakfast. She glanced up as Ricky entered, noting the sour expression on his face. "Well, I guess you're right," Ricky muttered as he walked in.

Anna, ever the humorist, laughed. "Of course, I'm right! You didn't marry Mrs. Right. You married Mrs. Always Right!" She expected Ricky to join her in laughter, but he remained somber.

She turned around, concerned by his unusual demeanor. "What happened?"

"Bart just bit my backside. I guess we'll have to sell him," Ricky replied, disheartened.

Anna's playful expression softened, replaced with concern. "Show me the bite mark." Ricky turned around, revealing the bite by his back pocket. But then Anna noticed something unusual.

Pulling a carrot from his back pocket, Anna held it up. "This has been here since last night. Bart was after this!"

Relieved, Ricky exclaimed, "Well, that makes me feel a lot better! He was after that carrot!"

Anna returned to serving breakfast, a smile tugging at her lips. "You won't need to sell Bart. Now, how about some breakfast?"

"Sounds good to me," Ricky said, washing his hands. "Then I can feed the rest of the animals."

Meanwhile, the mystery of the midnight singing played on Hattie's mind. She decided to go for a walk to the highest point of the island, hoping to uncover more clues.

Fredericksburg Island was 7.5 miles around, with rolling hills, tall grasses, majestic oak trees, and lush green bushes. The paths were unpaved, gravel and dirt winding through the idyllic landscape. Birds chirped merrily as Hattie made her way to the island's peak. There were no paved roads, only gravel and dirt paths. The island was home to various birds and one restaurant, Dairy Lane, on Main Street past the houses, stores, and a historic stone church from 1679.

Upon reaching the peak, Hattie had a clear, unobstructed view of the island. She pondered over the poem's words, "you talk of high, but you bow your head."

"I would bow my head as I'm looking down at everything," she thought. The next lines, "go down, down and around round instead," led her to take a trail descending towards the beach. She wondered if boulders that once existed there were now gone.

"Oh yes, ships come in but do not stay. So...some kind of port..." she murmured. Hattie took a right towards the main beach that faced Main Street.

Hattie continued her walk, admiring the quaint stone cottages and shops on Main Street, adorned with flowers. The island had farms, including Ricky and Anna's, and Carl and Hattie's, located near the church. The island was peaceful, with few residents who knew each other well.

Despite its tranquility, the island held excitement for a treasure hunt. Hattie needed to find where the port mentioned in the poem used to be.

As she walked along the beach, Hattie tripped over a rock and discovered an oval opening in the sand dunes. Peering inside with her flashlight, she found a tunnel stretching the length of the island.

Curiosity piqued, she ventured into the tunnel but decided not to explore its full length. Instead, she returned the way she came, eager to share her discovery with Carl over supper.

Chapter 10: The Treasure of the Hidden Tunnel

As the golden hues of the evening sun filtered through the kitchen window, Hattie busied herself preparing supper. The kitchen, with its warm, rustic charm, smelled of freshly baked bread and roasted vegetables. Just then, Carl walked in, curiosity painted on his weathered face. Despite the lines of age, his eyes still held a spark of adventure.

"Where did you go today?" he asked, his voice filled with genuine interest as he leaned against the doorframe.

"I went for a walk to find the treasure," Hattie replied, her eyes lighting up with excitement. She was a petite woman with a keen mind and an unyielding determination. "I think I have figured out some of the clues, but others still stump me. Down by the beach, I tripped over a rock hidden in the sand and found a tunnel. I believe it leads to the other side of the island."

Carl pondered for a moment, his brows furrowed in thought. "Hum. Is it far from here?" he asked, his voice tinged with concern.

"No, just down on the beach. Not too far," she answered, her hands busy spreading butter on a slice of warm bread.

Carl suggested they visit the spot together after dinner, and Hattie agreed eagerly. After their meal, they strolled down to the beach, the sand cool under their feet and the sound of waves crashing in the distance.

"See!" Hattie exclaimed, pointing to the tunnel hidden behind a cluster of rocks. "Right in there, this is the passageway I found. Pretty neat, huh!? You know the stories of tunnels and buried treasure. I bet that song led to the buried treasure in this passageway."

"This tunnel leads to the other side of the island," Carl observed, his voice steady but serious. "I don't think I want you to ever walk in this tunnel again."

Hattie was taken aback by Carl's stern tone. "Why?" she asked, her eyes searching his face for an answer.

"Just because. Just because. Let's go home and forget about all of this, plus it's getting dark now," Carl replied, a note of finality in his voice. His protective nature often clashed with Hattie's adventurous spirit, but it was rooted in deep care.

As they walked home, the twilight deepened into darkness, and they had to tread carefully. Suddenly, they heard their milk cow, Henrietta— Harrie for short—bellowing loudly. Forgetting about caution, they ran toward the commotion. Out of nowhere, something big and terrifying charged at them in the dark!

It hit Carl first, knocking him to the ground, and narrowly missed Hattie by inches. "Carl!" Hattie screamed, rushing to his side. "Are you alright?!" Her hands shook as she helped him to his feet.

Carl, with Hattie's help, got up and brushed himself off. "Yeah. What was that?! I couldn't see what it was in the dark," he said, wincing from the pain.

Hattie, still shaken, responded, "I don't know, it all happened so quick! Woosh! Then it was gone!"

"I'm going to check on Harrie," Carl said, holding his back in pain as they made their way to the corral.

"I'm coming with you," Hattie insisted, her voice firm. "Do you think that is what has been terrorizing our nights?!"

"Yep. At least we know it's not human," Carl replied, his tone reassuring yet serious.

"But it's a monster!" Hattie exclaimed, recalling the size of the creature.

"We need to set up a watch from now on and take care of this monster. We can't have a dangerous thing like that roaming our island," Carl resolved, determination in his eyes.

They found Harrie at the gate of her corral, bellowing with excitement. "There, there, girl," Carl soothed, petting her. "It's okay. Whatever that was, we scared it off for you."

"Is she safe?" Hattie asked, her voice tinged with worry. "You don't think the monster will come back tonight?"

"No, it's gone for now. Let's go to bed. My back hurts from that fall. I'm not as young as I used to be," Carl admitted with a tired sigh.

The next morning, after breakfast, Carl walked over to Ricky and Anna's farm to talk to Ricky about the monster encounter.

"Morning, Ricky," Carl greeted as he approached the barn.

Ricky turned from feeding the calves. "Morning, Carl! How are you?" he asked, noticing Carl's stiff movements.

"Not too good," Carl replied, wincing slightly.

"What's the problem? And why are you walking like you're hurting?" Ricky inquired, concern evident in his voice.

"We have a monster problem. Last night, something big and dark charged at me and knocked me down. It almost got Hattie too. We couldn't tell what it was in the dark, but it's not human. We need to set up a night watch until we get this taken care of," Carl explained, his tone serious.

"Yeah," Ricky agreed, taking off his hat and scratching his head. "We have women and the elderly to think of on this island. Okay, we'll start watching tonight."

"Can you watch until midnight tonight?" Carl asked. "Then I'll take over until morning."

"Yes, I can keep watch until midnight," Ricky confirmed. "Hopefully, we will get to the bottom of this soon. Hey! Before you go, you haven't seen our bull, Ollie."

Carl and Ricky walked to the back pasture to see Ollie. "This is Ollie? He sure is big," Carl remarked, reaching out to pet the massive bull.

"Yeah, I'll be glad when the shipment of heifers gets here," Ricky responded with a smile.

"When are they supposed to come?" Carl asked.

"I bought two. They should be here in a month," Ricky replied.

"Well, you know Ollie will be glad when they do get here." Carl chuckled as he petted the bull.

"Yep, he sure will enjoy the company," Ricky agreed, patting Ollie's side.

Chapter 11: The Hidden Tunnel

Anna stood at the sink, washing the last of the morning dishes. She was a petite woman in her early fifties, with a curious mind and an adventurous spirit. "I think I want to go treasure hunting right now," she mumbled to herself, her hazel eyes glinting with excitement. "I bet I can find it. Now what did that song say?" She furrowed her brow, trying to recall the lyrics. "Talk of high, but you bow your head. Talk of high would be..."

She turned to her husband, Ricky. He was a tall man with a rugged build and a knack for solving puzzles. "Hey Ricky, didn't you say there used to be a military fort here on the island?"

"Yep," Ricky replied, looking up from his book.

"And was there a lookout tower on the fort?"

"Yep. Just to the left of Main Street, before the beach. But it's been destroyed by storms. I guess the foundation is still there."

Anna's eyes lit up, and a smile spread across her face. "I'm going for a walk."

"Okay," Ricky said, grinning at her enthusiasm.

Anna walked past the quaint cottages and the small store that marked the center of their island community. The sun was shining brightly, casting a warm glow over the cobblestone streets. She reached the edge of Main Street and looked to the left, noticing the old tower foundation. "So, if I stand there, I would talk of high but look down and bow my head, and if it had spiral stairs, I would go down, down and around, round. Ships come in but do not stay..." She gazed at the crystal-clear water. "I don't see a port. Why wouldn't the ships stay? This is a protected spot."

To the left of the tower foundation, Anna spotted a hole partially hidden by sand dunes and tall grass. Intrigued, she walked over to inspect it. To her amazement, she discovered a tunnel entrance, large and lined with meticulously placed stones.

"Wow! I wonder if the vault is in here," she said aloud, her voice echoing slightly in the tunnel. Excitedly, she decided to go home, get Ricky, and fetch a flashlight.

Upon reaching the house, she burst through the door. "Guess what I found!"

Ricky could see the excitement in his wife's eyes. "What did you find?"

"I found one of those tunnels!" Anna exclaimed, barely able to contain her excitement.

"Where is it?" Ricky asked eagerly, setting his book aside.

"Just to the left of the old tower foundation. It's hidden by a sand dune and tall grass. I came back to get you and a flashlight. Do you want to go with me?"

"Sure!" Ricky said, jumping up and grabbing his flashlight. The two of them quickly set off for the place.

Arriving at the tunnel, Ricky shined his light into the entrance. "Wow! I never knew this was here. This is amazing! Look at the rock work!" He felt the texture of the stones as they slowly walked by them, marveling at the craftsmanship.

"It looks like there are different passages in here. I can't believe you found this!" Ricky said, turning to Anna with a look of admiration.

"I know!" Anna replied, her voice filled with excitement. "What if it leads us to the treasure?!"

"Well, the crow had to get the two coins from somewhere. Maybe he found it in here," Ricky suggested, pointing out a few bird's nests in the tunnel. Taking Anna's hand, he said, "Let's go a little further in and stay close to me."

The two took their time exploring the tunnel, their footsteps echoing softly on the brick floor. "It looks like this goes on for miles," Anna commented, her eyes wide with wonder.

"I bet it does," Ricky agreed. "Look at all the different passages. Someone worked hard on this structure. The stone walls are perfect, no damage. I don't think anyone has been here in years."

"It feels like a cave with vaulted ceilings and whitewashed walls, but the flooring is all brick. I wonder where we are on the island in this spot. Was this part of the fort?" Anna asked, looking around in awe.

"I don't know," Ricky said, his voice filled with curiosity. "Hey, we need to get back to the farm, and don't you have dinner with Carl and Hattie tonight at the Dairy Lane?"

"Yep. I guess we better go back for now. But can we come back and look further?" Anna asked, her voice tinged with eagerness.

"Yeah, we'll come back and bring food and water so we can take all day and explore," Ricky promised, giving her hand a reassuring squeeze.

As they walked back to the house, Anna asked, "Are you standing guard tonight to see if you can catch the monster?"

"Yep. I'm going to sit on the rock wall facing the pasture between our place and Carl's. It seems that's where the most activity has been. First, Pastor Tower got knocked down at our rock wall, and then Carl and I, found footprints from our place to theirs. Carl and Hattie were attacked at their place. So, I think sitting on the stone wall would be a good spot."

"Well, you be careful," Anna cautioned, her voice filled with concern. "We don't need you getting hurt. I mean, you already got bit," she added with a laugh.

Ricky grinned at her. "You be careful walking back in the dark without me holding you up. Don't fall down."

"Yeah, yeah, yeah," Anna said, grinning back. "It's not you holding me up, it's me holding you up. Do you want me to bring something back from the restaurant?" she asked.

"Pick me up a burger meal and drink," Ricky replied as Anna went to get ready for dinner, and he prepared to guard the stone wall.

Later, as Ricky sat listening to the crickets singing, he saw Carl and Hattie walking from their farm to his. The night was cool, and the stars twinkled brightly above.

"Hello, Ricky!" Carl greeted him, his voice breaking the quiet.

"Hi Carl!" Ricky replied.

"We thought we would walk with Anna to the Dairy Lane since you are taking the first watch. We don't want her walking alone with this thing attacking people," Hattie explained, her tone protective.

"I appreciate that. Thank you. She's about ready. I'm geared up to catch this thing causing trouble. Hopefully, tonight we can put an end to this and have peaceful nights again," Ricky said, determination in his voice.

"Yeah, I'm ready to get back to normal too," Carl agreed.

"Come on Carl, let's get Anna and go eat. Do you want us to bring you back some food from the restaurant?" Hattie asked.

"Anna is already bringing me back some food, but thank you for thinking of me," Ricky said, feeling touched by their concern.

"Be careful. We don't need anybody else getting hurt," Hattie cautioned, her voice serious.

"I will, don't worry. It's probably nothing too bad," Ricky reassured her.

"I don't know Ricky, it hit me pretty hard. I'm still hurting. Just be careful," Carl advised, concern evident in his voice.

"Have fun at the restaurant," Ricky said, feeling a bit left out.

"Bye!" Carl and Hattie said together as they went to pick up Anna.

Anna walked out and over to Ricky. "Bye, honey. I'll bring you back a burger meal," she promised, giving him a quick kiss.

"Thank you," Ricky said, watching her walk away with Carl and Hattie.

Even though Ricky wasn't with them, Anna, Carl, and Hattie enjoyed a good meal but kept wondering about Ricky.

"Well, the time has gone by fast. It's already eight o'clock. I better get the food to Ricky so he can eat," Anna said, checking her watch.

"Hattie and I will walk with you. I want to see if your husband has spotted our monster yet," Carl said. "And we don't feel right letting you walk alone in the dark."

"Now don't you start," Anna laughed. "I'm the one who keeps Ricky up."

"Sure you are," Carl and Hattie said together, laughing.

As they approached the Stehling farm, Anna voiced her concern to Hattie. "I wonder if Ricky has spotted anything yet."

"I did!" Ricky's voice startled them all.

All three jumped, their hearts racing.

No one had seen Ricky standing against the rock wall of the house in the dark.

"Where did you come from?! You scared the tar out of me!" Anna reprimanded him, her voice shaky.

Hattie was laughing hard. "I almost wet my pants!"

"What did you see?" Carl asked, ignoring the women's excitement.

"Well, you won't believe me if I told you. So, I have to show you. Can you and Hattie come for dinner tomorrow?" Ricky asked, a mysterious glint in his eye.

"Yeah, Hattie, is that okay?" Carl asked his wife.

"Yep," she said.

"Okay, well all I'm going to say is you have to see it to believe it. Oh, and you're safe to walk home tonight. Nothing is going to attack you," Ricky assured them.

"Good to know! See you guys tomorrow night," Carl called as they started for their farm.

"Okay! Good night!" Ricky and Anna called back. Turning to his wife, Ricky said, "So I scared you,

Ana turning towards her husband with a smile said," you know you did!"

Chapter 12: Mystery monster

It was a warm, spring day with a gentle breeze coming off the ocean. The sky was a deep blue with no clouds to block the sun. Birds sang joyfully, filling the trees with their melodies.

Anna, a woman with a green thumb and a love for gardening, was kneeling in her flower beds, her sunhat shielding her from the bright rays. Her husband, Ricky, a curious and adventurous soul, was puttering around the farm, fixing fences and tending to the animals.

"Hey, honey, have you checked that bird's nest in the barn lately for any more coins?" Anna called out, her voice carrying across the yard.

Ricky, wiping sweat from his brow, looked up. "Let's go look now," he replied, a hint of excitement in his voice.

They walked together to the barn, their steps crunching on the gravel path. Reaching the nest, they found one more coin, its metallic glint catching the light.

"I wonder where that crow is finding these coins. Maybe it's in the tunnel where we were," Anna mused, turning the coin over in her hand, her eyes sparkling with curiosity.

"I don't know, but I'd sure like to find out," Ricky said, his mind already racing with possibilities. "Can you pack us a lunch? I'll grab some water, and we can head back to the tunnel. I don't have anything urgent until this evening, do you?"

"No, I just need to make dinner for tonight, but I can do that later," Anna agreed, her excitement matching his. "We're going to have seven-layer dip and chips, so it'll be easy. Let's go!"

With their flashlights, a light lunch, and bottles of water, Anna and Ricky ventured back to the tunnel. The air was cool and damp as they descended, the beam of their flashlights cutting through the darkness.

"Golly! I hope we find the treasure down here," Anna exclaimed, her voice echoing off the stone walls.

Ricky started humming an old rhyme, his deep voice resonating. "Talk of high, but you bow your head..."

Anna pondered, "I thought of the tower. Maybe they had a spiral staircase?"

"I don't know," Ricky replied, scratching his head. "But why would ships come in but not stay? It doesn't match, does it?"

"No, it doesn't," Anna sighed, her disappointment evident.

They continued exploring the tunnel until they came to a wall with a door. Anna's curiosity got the better of her. "Let's look inside and see what's in there," she urged.

"Probably nothing. This whole structure has been empty," Ricky said skeptically.

To their amazement, the room was full of clay jars and bottles, all bearing the year 1679.

"Holly cow! Look at this!" Ricky exclaimed, his flashlight illuminating the ancient jars.

"These things have been here for years! No one knows about them," Anna marveled, running her fingers over the dusty surfaces.

"What a find. This is so amazing!" Ricky exclaimed, his excitement growing. "They've been shut up in this storeroom for centuries. This must have been part of the fort. Look at the wine bottles. The wine is still in them. There are clay jars here. I bet that was spices. Let's look in the boxes."

They quickly opened the boxes, finding utensils, oils, and other supplies. "It's kitchen supplies. I think we are near where the kitchen was at the fort. This is where they stored the kitchen supplies," Anna deduced.

"Well, let's close the door and head back home," Ricky suggested. "We will come back another time."

"Maybe we can find more stuff that we could send to the fort museum on the mainland," Anna said, her eyes shining with excitement.

"Sounds good to me," Ricky agreed.

Back at the farm, Anna busied herself preparing a delicious seven-layer dip and a cream key lime pie for their friends Carl and Hattie, who were coming for dinner. She was getting antsy to solve the mystery of the monster that Ricky had been teasing her about.

As they sat down to eat, Hattie whispered to Anna, "Did Ricky tell you what the mystery monster was?"

Anna shook her head and rolled her eyes. "No. He just keeps saying you got to see it to believe it!"

"Well, I for one will be happy to put all of this to rest," Carl said matter-of-factly.

After dinner, Ricky announced, "It's getting dark outside. Shall we all go?"

The group anxiously followed Ricky to the rock wall facing the back pasture gate. Ricky whispered, "Now everybody remain quiet and follow me. When we get to the rock wall, just sit down and watch the gate to the pasture."

They all sat down quietly, their eyes fixed on the gate. Suddenly, the latch on the gate rattled, and to their astonishment, out walked Ollie the bull! He closed the gate behind him by pushing it closed with his back side, and trotted off to Carl and Hattie's farm.

Everyone's mouths dropped open in amazement. The mystery was solved, "Come on, this isn't all of it," Ricky said, motioning for everyone to follow.

They got up and followed Ollie at a distance. Ollie never looked their way; he just kept going. When they reached Carl and Hattie's place, Ricky stopped everyone at the corner of the house. They all peered around the corner and watched Ollie court Herrietta, the cow.

"Well! I never!" Hattie whispered, her eyes wide with surprise.

"A love-sick bull," Carl whispered back to his wife, shaking his head in disbelief.

Ricky motioned for the group to huddle a little closer. "This isn't everything. Hang on, it gets better," he whispered.

As they watched from their hiding place, they saw Ollie make a turn and walk back to his pasture.

"Come on," Ricky urged.

They all followed Ollie again back to the gate. They stood at a distance and watched as Ollie used his tongue to open the latch, walked into his pen, turned around, and grabbed a rope tied to the gate to close it behind him.

Everyone's mouths were open in disbelief once again.

"Well, I would have never guessed that Ollie is a Romeo!" Anna said softly, shaking her head.

"Ollie and Herrietta are in love," Hattie said, a smile spreading across her face.

"This is our monster that knocked me down?" Carl asked, still in shock.

"And Pastor Tower down," Ricky added. "I got to thinking it all happened in just this area. So, I sat on the wall and was watching. Obviously, Ollie did not see me sitting there. When it got dark after all of you were in the restaurant, I was sitting here quietly and heard the gate rattle. That drew my attention towards Ollie. I watched him use his tongue to open the latch on the gate. Then he went walking towards your place, and I followed him at a distance. When I got to your farm, I saw that he was courting Herrietta through her fence. He didn't stay long and did what he did tonight turned around and walked back to our farm. As I watched, I stood in the field and saw how he used that rope to close the gate behind him. I knew you would not believe me if I told you. So, you had to see it for yourself. We don't have a monster problem. We have a love story."

Carl, still in total disbelief, said, "Well, I have meant to talk to you about using Ollie for our cow. We need a calf so we can get milk. I guess it's nice they already like each other."

"Oh, how sweet. Ollie and Herrietta are in love," Hattie said, her eyes twinkling.

"I think it's all so romantic," Anna said. "Just proves you can't keep true love apart."

Ricky shook his head and said, "Okay, don't get too carried away now."

Everyone laughed.

Carl was still trying to figure out the whole story. "Wait, Ollie hit me hard! I went flying. Why did he do that?"

Ricky leaned against the fence and said, "I thought about that. Do you remember you heard Herrietta bellowing and then you came running?"

"Yeah, that's what happened," Carl replied.

"Ollie is a scaredy-cat. He runs and hides when something runs at him."

"So, what you're saying is I scared him?!" Carl persisted.

"Yep. He was trying to run away from you, but you were in his way! You were his bogeyman."

"So, our favorite milk cow was bellowing because we interrupted their courting?" Hattie asked.

"That or Ollie wasn't paying her much attention. She was trying to get his attention on her, then he got scared and ran away, and she was upset about that," Ricky explained.

Anna said, "You messed their date up. I would be upset too if my date got messed up."

"What about Pastor Tower? Why did Ollie knock him down?" Carl asked.

"My thought is," Ricky said, "When Pastor Tower was here, it was dark, and Ollie was off to see Herrietta. Somehow, Pastor Tower must've made a noise and scared Ollie. Ollie started to run and collided into him from behind, knocking Pastor Tower down."

"Well, I'll be!" Carl exclaimed.

"And yes, before anyone asks, starting tonight there will be a chain and a lock on that gate," Ricky announced. Everyone laughed, relieved that the mystery was finally solved.

WELL!